MAN-MAN
AND THE
TREE OF
MEMORIES

ALSO BY THE AUTHOR
FOR OLDER READERS

A Jigsaw of Fire and Stars
Wolf Light
Lionheart Girl

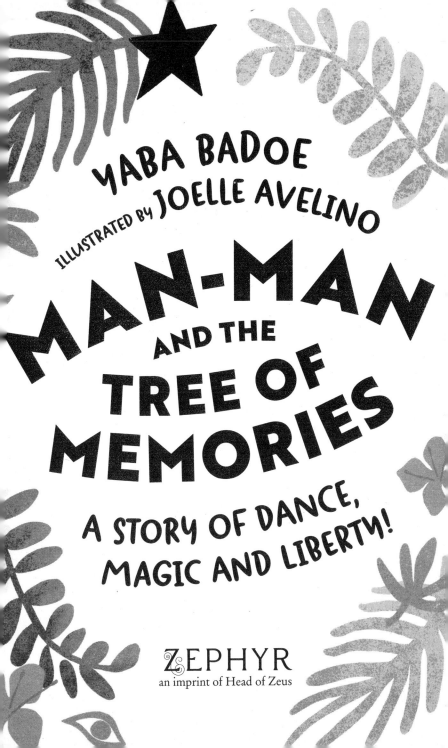

YABA BADOE

ILLUSTRATED BY JOELLE AVELINO

MAN-MAN
AND THE
TREE OF
MEMORIES

A STORY OF DANCE, MAGIC AND LIBERTY!

ZEPHYR
an imprint of Head of Zeus

This is a Zephyr book first published in the UK in 2023 by Head of Zeus Ltd
This edition first published in 2025 by Head of Zeus Ltd,
part of Bloomsbury Publishing Plc

9 7 5 3 1 2 4 6 8

A catalogue record for this book is available from the British Library.

ISBN (PB): 9781035912605
ISBN (eBook): 9781837930050

Designed by Jessie Price

Printed and bound in Great Britain by
CPI Group (UK) Ltd, Croydon CR0 4YY

Bloomsbury Publishing Plc
50 Bedford Square, London, WC1B 3DP, UK
Bloomsbury Publishing Ireland Limited,
29 Earlsfort Terrace, Dublin 2, D02 AY28, Ireland

HEAD OF ZEUS LTD
5–8 Hardwick Street, London EC1R 4RG

To find out more about our authors and books visit www.headofzeus.com
For product safety related questions contact productsafety@bloomsbury.com

To revellers of the past, present and future,
especially my grandchildren, Nii Armah, Lael,
Laurel, Leuan, Joseph, and Rowan.

– YB

To the joys and celebrations of carnival,
and the people that make it happen –
thank you for continuing the magic.

– JA

ONCE, not so long ago, there lived a boy whose mother was suffering from an illness no one could name. Doctors and healers of all kinds couldn't explain what was wrong with her. Neither could they understand why, as she grew thinner and thinner, her voice started to fade.

The boy's name was Man-man, and his home was in London in a part of the city famous for its yearly carnival.

Late one afternoon, soon after his mum had taken to her bed, Man-man was practising his steps for carnival when a voice from the kitchen yelled: 'De pickney dem today *always* making noise! Man-man, why you thumping and strumming? Why you *stomping* your feet on the ground?'

The voice belonged to his nan.

Fedora Roberts had arrived from Jamaica that morning to look after her daughter, Trilby, Man-man's mum.

Man-man froze between steps, clenching his fingers to stop them teasing music out of the tables and walls around him. 'Today is *dread*,' he muttered.

Not only was his mum ill, she was wobbly on her feet as well. So wobbly she could barely walk. What's more, her voice was almost gone. That's why Dad had called Nan and begged her to come over.

That's how bad things were, for his dad didn't much like Nan. 'She too prissy-prim for her own good,' he always said.

Unable to practise in silence on wooden floorboards, Man-man slipped off his shoes and moving his weight from foot to foot, heel to toe, glided down the corridor. He tweaked his shoulders and hips, jerking his neck from side to side, until, twitching like a robot, he reached his parents' room.

His dad was still at work at his

barber shop while Pan, Man-man's older sister, was out with friends. Pan hadn't returned home since Nan's arrival. Neither had her tortoise shell cat, Smudge, who, more often than not, followed Pan's example.

Man-man tapped on the bedroom door and stepped inside.

'There you are,' his mum murmured. 'The minute I think of you, you come!' She smiled, a smile that tickled his skin like a prickle of sunlight in winter. A smile that made him grin, even though Nan had told him to leave his mum in peace.

'I have travelled *all* the way to England,' Nan had said when she'd seen the state they were in.

Clothes strewn on the washing machine clamoured to be washed.

A heap of takeaway cartons littered the kitchen. Smudge, nestling among them, snarled.

In the sitting room Nan had run a finger along a shelf before flicking specks of dust in the air.

'I have travelled all the way to England,' she repeated, 'to make sure that your mother rests. I will cook and clean and take care of you on one condition. You'll do what I say.'

Pan's eyes had flung daggers at Nan. Daggers that said: *I am nobody's slave.*

She'd flung daggers, then flounced out, Smudge behind her; while Dad, looking grim, had followed.

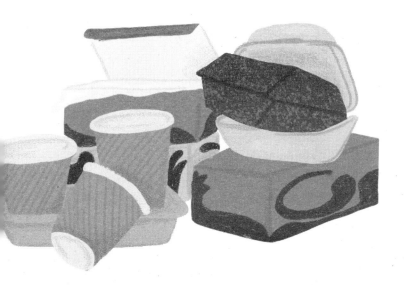

Unfortunately for Man-man, once Nan's eyes had drilled into his, he couldn't move. Even in his parents' room, he could still hear her voice and the furious squeak in it as she'd waggled a finger at him.

The finger seemed to jab him, for he took a step back. Yet, as soon as his mum lifted her duvet, with a skip and a jump, Man-man snuggled into her bed.

Fuzzy with sleep, she stroked his cheek and slowly inhaled him, as if his smell reminded her of all the things she loved and missed most in the world. She lapped him up like a camel drinking water after a long desert trek. Her forehead touched his, and Man-man gazed at his mum's face.

The plump curves of her cheeks had gone. Her eyes were dull with pain. And yet the more he stared into those dark eyes of hers, the more his mind tricked him.

Instead of seeing her as she was, he saw her as she used to be, how he wanted her to be: bigger, louder, healthier than ever; the very best mum in the world.

'You're snugalicious,' she whispered.

'You're snugalicious too.'

She held him, and breathing him in again and again, soft as a butterfly settling on his hand, she asked, 'I heard you practising. Have you got it?'

He nodded.

All day long he'd been distracted because he was

busy working on his steps for carnival. This year at Notting Hill, he was going to take his mum's place and lead the procession. Pan would be at his side. He'd listen to the beat of his dad's sound system, feel the rhythm, and, when he was in its groove, he'd move.

'Will you dance me better, Man-man?'

'I'll dance you to the moon and back, Mum,' he promised. 'To infinity and beyond!'

'Wouldn't surprise me,' she smiled. 'You were dancing when you were small as a grub inside me, little man. We've been dancing ever since.'

This was a story his mum often told him.

And it was when she and Dad had started calling him Man-man. He was their little man, though his real name was Emmanuel.

'Is your costume ready?'

Man-man nodded again.

Aunty Flo, a designer and seamstress, had been working on their costumes for ages. 'You can be anyone you want to be at carnival,' she'd said.

'A bird, a queen, a troubadour, a warrior.

For one day and one day
only, you can decide who you
are and feel it deep down. Who will you be this
year, Man-man?'

He'd whispered in her ear and grinned as her
eyes sparkled.

'Mind the Queen of Revels doesn't nab you,
boy,' she'd warned. 'Because once I've dressed you
up, all eyes will be on *you*. And where we look, the
eyes of the Revel Queen follow.'

In truth, it wasn't just what he wanted to be for
a day that mattered. All the troupe had had a say.
One after the other they'd suggested a theme and
then voted. This year they'd chosen 'Let Freedom
Rain'. They were going to celebrate the freedom
of Africans everywhere – from Port-au-Prince to
London, Solihull to Salvador, Cape Town to Cairo,
Zanzibar to Spanish Town, Jamaica. At the same
time, they were going to honour freedom fighters of
yesterday, such as Queen Nanny, Marcus Garvey,
Toussaint Louverture, Jean-Jacques Dessalines,

Martin Luther King and Yaa Asantewaa of Ghana.

His mum gathered her strength before speaking again.

Having learned how to catch the softest of her words, Man-man was ready when her question fluttered into the open. 'Who are you going to be at carnival this year?'

He caught her drift even though she sounded far away like someone lost in fog. What flummoxed him was the breathlessness between her pauses. With each gasp he felt the tug of his mum slipping away. A tug that wiped the smile off his face and brought tears to his eyes.

'My costume's a secret,' Man-man replied.

'You're not going to go as the Black Panther, are you?'

Outside a floorboard creaked.

Trilby placed a finger to her lips.

The doorknob turned. The door swung open, and Nan appeared.

A small woman with a round, pert face, she glared at Man-man, her eyebrow raised, and what at first seemed ordinary became extraordinarily large. Large like an orchestra of clashing cymbals and shaking tambourines. Nan loomed, an ogre, skin pale as topaz, a smattering of salt and pepper curls on her scalp.

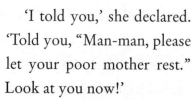

'I told you,' she declared. 'Told you, "Man-man, please let your poor mother rest." Look at you now!'

His mum drew him closer.

'Fedora, I called him. See how bright he's made me?'

'But, Trilby, we agreed…'

'We did. But this is my time, Ma, and I need to spend it with my son.'

Nan nodded, even as her face fixed in a frown.

Once she was gone, Trilby tickled Man-man, whispering: ''Fess up, son. True, true, you've asked Flo to dress you up as the Black Panther, haven't you?'

Man-man snorted. That had been his first choice, until his dad had pointed out that the kingdom of Wakanda was a make-believe creation of Marvel Comics and that T'Challa wasn't a *genuine* freedom fighter. Jules had explained patiently, while Pan and her pals had sniggered, teasing Man-man that the one African country he was desperate to visit didn't exist. He remembered the glance Pan had thrown him. How he'd shrivelled inside at what she could do to him with that glint in her eyes.

'Mum, like I said, my costume's a secret. You'll have to come to carnival to find out who I am, because before I can dance you better, you have to be well enough to watch.'

'So, I've got two weeks to mend body and soul and walk again?'

'You can do it, Mum. I know you can do it.'

THE FORTNIGHT before carnival disappeared in a flurry of costume fittings and rehearsals. The Let Freedom Rain crew spent hours rigging a float, while drummers and dancers prepared for the big day.

This was the fortnight in which Man-man and Pan perfected their moves: high kicks, belly rolls, the limbo stroll. They practised dancing side by side, and then thighs wide apart, they strutted, bottoms gyrating like bundles of bouncing balls. Finally, arms outstretched, back to back, they waggled their legs before slip-sliding in splits.

The more they practised, and their mum heard the stamp of feet followed by their laughter, the more determined she became to see her children perform.

Day after day, what had seemed impossible to begin with glimmered, giving Man-man hope that if she could only see him lead the procession, he would be able to dance her back to good health. Her eyes were brighter now, and smiles flitted over her face.

Much of this was thanks to Nan's cooking. She created spinach and coconut milk smoothies, conjured mango and pumpkin pies. She whipped up endless chicken and vegetable broths, scrumptious dumplings on top; cups of soup followed by bowls of curried goat and callaloo.

After marinading delicate morsels of fish, she baked corn bread and fish patties to entice her daughter to eat.

No wonder Trilby's cheeks were beginning to fill out again. As the flesh around her bones became fatter, she grew louder; so that when she spoke, her voice was no longer as faint as drops of rain falling on the sea, but strong as a tide surging in.

His mum was getting better. Man-man felt it and was convinced by what he saw. So much so, that on the day Trilby was able to stagger into the sitting room to watch them, even though she was holding the walls to keep herself upright, brother and sister clapped, delighted.

In the kitchen, the buzz of Nan grumbling erupted in a clatter of pots and pans. Between the clanging of lids, snatches of what she was saying rolled into the sitting room.

'Downtown wickedness,' she hissed.

Smudge leaped from the kitchen to the sitting room.

'To come
to England,' Nan
droned, 'to see my own
flesh and blood swaying their
backsides like dancehall queens! Mercy
me!'

Saucepans crashed as Nan's temper flamed.

'Let her be, Mum,' Pan whispered. 'You know what Nan's like.'

Trilby nodded. Yet before Pan could distract her, or Man-man could douse Nan's temper by giving her a hug, Trilby choked. Once, twice, she spluttered. Each time she thumped her chest to clear her throat. After a third wallop, a sound like a mouse scuttling over autumn leaves emerged. 'Ma,' she asked, 'what's your problem?'

Hands on hips, Nan strode into the sitting room.

'Daughter, no one could ever call me a saint, but I'm not a prude.'

'Oh, yes, you are,' Pan mumbled.

Smudge spat, winding her body between Pan's legs.

Nan replied with a look that should have shredded girl and cat. Not Panama. Or Smudge. Back hunched, the cat hissed while the girl sneered. Head raised, her pose mirrored Fedora's exactly.

Disgusted.

Defiant.

A duo, daggers drawn.

Nan harrumphed: 'Daughter, since my eyes were at my knees, me never see what me see day after day in this house. All this strutting and wobbling and belly rolling make me think me not in England, but in a den of thieves in downtown Kingston. Hip-shaking in a boy is bad enough. But shakey-shake in a girl? No, daughter, no!'

'But, Nan, we're *practising*,' Man-man explained. 'Practising for carnival.'

He looked from Nan to his mum and back again. Anger glittered in their eyes as their passion scorched Man-man's skin.

Trilby gulped more air. Hit her chest again. Then, to Man-man's alarm, she coughed up a tiny, white feather. It fluttered to the ground.

'Mum, what's happening to you?' he cried.

Was the feather goose down from her duvet? Had she got out of bed too soon? Man-man didn't know. How could he when Smudge's caterwauling made it impossible to think?

No one seemed to have noticed the feather but him. He picked it up and put it in his pocket convinced that Trilby wasn't well enough to be up.

Meanwhile, the daggers duo circled each other, panthers about to pounce.

'Ma, these are *my* children, they follow *my* rules. We're about to celebrate carnival. What better way to express love of life and freedom than by dancing?'

'Dancing? You call jerking and twerking *dancing*?'

'Mother.' Trilby lowered her voice so that everyone except for Man-man had to lean in to hear what she was saying. 'Mother,' she repeated. 'This is my house, my children. I feel better with you here, really, I do. Even so, you will not impose the rules you caged me with as a pickney on my children. We're not uptown in Stony Hill now. We're in Ladbroke Grove where at carnival we celebrate who we are, African roots and all.'

'Carnival, barnacle!' Nan scoffed. 'All that talk of "Africa" nothing but Rasta nonsense. Remember Grandma Gatsby? Remember how she took to her bed with the same sickness you have, Trilby? And then when she couldn't talk, she choked on a feather? Carnival did it.'

Trilby sighed.

'Daughter, if you prance about like the pickney dem you may as well dance with the devil. And if you do that you'll go to a place where your tongue can't move and there's no coming back.'

Man-man rubbed his ear, puzzled. Nobody wanted *that*. Not even Kareem, his best friend, who made a point of liking things other kids didn't. For example, instead of tucking into burgers and fries, Kareem relished tofu and vegetables, anchovies and olives. He even liked runny cheese. Kareem didn't want to go to a place where his tongue couldn't move and neither did Man-man. But the

idea that *dancing* could take him there, and that his great-grandma, Gatsby had suffered as a result of carnival, were completely new.

He blinked at Nan, amazed she thought a gift he enjoyed, that his mum encouraged, was *dangerous*. It didn't make sense until, remembering what Aunty Flo had said to him, Man-man asked: 'Is the Revel Queen evil, Nan? Will her eyes be on us at carnival?'

''Course not, silly,' said Pan. 'It's all make-believe, same as the kingdom of Wakanda and the Black Panther!'

'Nonsense,' Nan snapped. 'Wickedness is real, boy. And whether it's in the form of a man or a woman, it's everywhere. Your great-grandma, Gatsby found that out to her peril. Ask your pa.'

'Dad?'

'That's enough, Fedora,' said Trilby. 'Don't say another word…'

Nan paused.

Grimaced.

Pursed her lips.

But when Pan started sniggering, irritation got the better of her.

'Believe me, Man-man,' said Nan. 'Danger at carnival is as real as these grey hairs on my head. You're too young to understand, but the three ugly sisters of sin are vices so hideous, you should have no toleration of them whatsoever. There's nothing in the world as ugly as alcohol, dancing and revelry. And when you put the three together,' Nan clapped her hands, 'wickedness soon come. If you dance like you've been doing here for carnival – wickedness will catch you and mash you up.'

NEXT DAY, with only two days left, Man-man jumped into a barber's chair at his dad's shop. Jules Baptiste was one of the most sought-after stylists in London. He cut the hair of both men and women, but mostly men – musicians and artists of all sorts – beat a path to his door. At Jules's they enjoyed mingling with everyday folk who dropped by to chat.

Legs outstretched, Man-man spun the chair. 'Ready for lift-off, partner?'

'Ready, Captain…'

Behind Man-man Kareem was pretending to co-pilot a spaceship built for intergalactic travel.

'Three, two, one, zero. Ignition, and we're off.'

Even as they soared and even though Pan was

out with Nan having her hair styled in a weave, that didn't stop Man-man hearing her voice.

Today, the Big Sister voice whispered: *Why can't you be friends with a regular dude, bro? Someone who isn't even weirder than you are, and sets my nerd alert off every single time?*

Pan's presence rarely left Man-man. But it didn't stop him doing what he wanted. If anything, it made him more determined, especially when it came to Kareem. They were more than best friends. Nicknamed Tall and Small at school because Kareem was long and lanky, while Man-man was small for his age, they were friends of the heart, who stuck to each other like limpets to rock.

Kareem, getting ready for carnival as well, wanted a buzz cut to sharpen his look – that of a pirate. He grinned at the thought of it. Grinned, as their spaceship arched over the Milky Way.

'Ground control to Man-man. Careful…' Jules's

hand stopped the chair spinning. In a heartbeat, he raised the seat, and after tying a sheaf of plastic around Man-man's neck, he smiled at him in the mirror. 'What's it to be this time, son?'

Man-man pointed at a photograph. Beside a painting of African men's hairstyles from the last century, the photo was of a model, a stud earring in the lobe of his ear. 'That's what I want, please, Dad.'

'A low skin fade,' said Jules, naming the style.

What appealed to Man-man was that running through the fade was a design of a flash of lightning in a stormy sky. It reminded him of the strange stories his dad told him about growing up in Haiti; stories about Dad's pa, and the tales he'd once told him about the god of thunder and lightning. 'They call him Shango,' Dad had said. 'And in his hand he holds a mighty axe!'

Man-man was thrilled as Jules started recreating the style on his scalp. He felt the sizzle and purr of the trimmer on his head and over his crown.

Jules tilted Man-man's head.

'All right, son?'

'Dad…' Man-man paused, trying to ask a question he'd been mulling over since he'd clambered into Mum's bed.

Perched in the waiting area of the salon, Kareem looked up from a comic, then turned a page.

'Go on,' said Jules. 'I'm listening.'

'Mum's going to get better, isn't she?'

'Course, she is!'

Jules spoke too quickly. 'She *will* get better. Having Nan around is helping. Haven't you noticed that Mum's cheeks are filling out? She's beginning to walk as well.'

'But her voice is disappearing again. The other day she coughed up a feather. A *feather*, Dad!'

'Must have been fluff. A bit of fluff, that's what she told me.'

Man-man shook his head.

'I saw it, Dad. I can

hardly hear her
any more. It's
like she's far
away somewhere,
talking to me
through thick fog.'

'Healing takes
time, son.'

Razor at the ready,
Jules began to create a flash
of lightning on the side of Man-
man's head. Gradually, a bolt of light
appeared in a Z of skin. The longer the bolt
became, the more an urge to begin the task he'd set
himself stirred in Man-man. He was going to find
his mum in the fog and dance her back to the light.

'I know Nan's helping, Dad,' he said. 'I know
she's trying her best, but she winds Mum up
something awful. She can't help herself.'

'I reckon that's just the way your grandmother
is,' Jules replied.

'Why's Nan the way she is?'

The design in place, Jules dabbed cologne on

Man-man's hairline. Above and behind his ears, the top of his neck. 'You remember that conversation we had about why the women in our family are named after hats?'

Man-man nodded.

For years he hadn't realised how odd this was. He couldn't be expected to know the word for every hat in the world, could he? For example, if Panama had been called Beret, or Trilby's name was Beanie, he'd have twigged long ago. As it was, when it dawned on him that his sister and Mum and Nan, as well as his great-grandmother, Gatsby, were named after head coverings, of course he'd asked: '*Why?*'

Pan had growled at his question, and roared: ''Cause we four is MIGHTY, lil' bro. And when we glare at you with the full blast of our eyes, small boys like you wither.'

'I remember,' he said. How could he forget, when a glance from Pan could cut him to the quick? 'Is Nan worse than Pan?'

Jules laughed. 'Same family, same blessings, same old curse. No other women that I know can throw shade with their eyes like our three can. I'm told it was the same with Great-Grandma Gatsby and, even way back before her. All the daughters of that family the same.'

'Great-Grandma as well? The grandma who died from the same illness Mum has?'

'She didn't die, Man-man. Gatsby took to her bed and simply stopped talking. The way I understand it, son, their names are supposed to protect us as much as it does them.'

'But how?'

'Think about it,' said Jules. 'Imagine the four of them together. Gatsby as well. If you can imagine them wearing the hats they're named after, the chance of anyone disrespecting them is almost zero. No one can see their anger, no one can accuse them of casting an evil eye. That's what your mum once told me. Their names are like a shield, a good luck charm to protect them and us.'

'But it doesn't work, Dad! The other day they were at each other like piranhas at a sniff of blood. It was crazy. Crazy. Pan was annoying Nan, and Mum couldn't talk. She kept walloping her chest. Since then, she's hardly spoken. Not properly. Not like she used to. It's as if her voice is buried inside her, and she can't dig it out.'

Man-man gulped, remembering. 'And Nan hates carnival. Hates the way Pan and I dance. She said, "Talk of Africa nothing but Rasta nonsense." Dad, she trashed everything you've taught us.' He puffed out his chest, copying his grandmother's panther-woman pose. 'Then she said, "Evil is real, boy. And whether it's in the shape of a man or a woman, at carnival it's everywhere. Great-Grandma Gatsby went to carnival and suffered. Ask your pa."'

Before his dad could reply, more questions hurtled from Man-man. 'Is her truth-telling for real? Is it true that if I perform at carnival and smash it with my best moves, the Revel Queen and wickedness will catch me and mash me up?'

If it's possible to sigh and laugh at the same time, Jules did. He chortled, amused yet exasperated. 'Fedora a woman of strong opinions, Man-man. She a woman with a will that cannot yield. A hard-headed woman with a skull tough as an old nanny goat.

'Like I said, blessings and curses. What some people call a curse,' said Jules, 'for example what happened to Great-Grandma Gatsby, I think of as the past trying to talk to us; the past trying to tell us something we need to know. It's a bit like when I play a track of music again and again. Eventually, I hear something new in it that helps me see it in a different light. Same old, same old. Then, *fresh eyes.*'

Man-man wasn't convinced. 'Why did Nan say what she did, though? Why did she want me to ask *you* about the bad things that happen at carnival?'

Jules pursed his lips. At last, he said, 'OK. You asked for it, so here it is. Tell me, do you see any difference between my skin and Nan's?'

'You're darker than she is. You're darker than Mum too. Darker than Pan. But you and me, we're the same.' Man-man stretched out his forearm and compared it to his dad's.

'Exactly. The fact is, because my skin is darker than Nan's, because she lives uptown in Kingston and I'm from a raggle-taggle village in Haiti. Because the best thing in the world to me is to smash it at carnival – where I met your mum – your nan can't abide me or carnival. In her heart of hearts, Nan thinks she's better than me.'

'She isn't better than you!'

'I know, I know,' said Jules. 'But deep down, that's what she believes. She told me.'

'Why?'

'Why does anyone think they're better than someone else?' Jules leaned into his son and caressed his cheek. 'I'm not saying it doesn't hurt. It does. But this I do know. While me and my folks went down to the river to pray, Fedora set herself on a church pew. Carnival is where Trilby tipped her hat at me and danced into my heart. And there she's stayed. She in mine; me in hers.

'That's our story, son. I'm from a village in Haiti. I'm a roots man, Haitian-style. An African who believes in roots magic: the magic of sea and sky, the wisdom of plants and trees, the strength of those who came before us and carry us back to Africa. Your grandmother thinks all of that is evil. I disagree.'

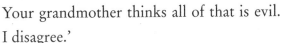

'Me too,' said Man-man.

Even though he didn't fully grasp what his dad was saying, he was more determined than ever to dance so well for his mum, he'd help her find her voice again.

AT LAST carnival day arrived. By the time revellers started gathering at the lock-up where the float was kept, the sun was nibbling its way through rain clouds. Before long, rays of sunshine peeped out, and lifting a veil of gloom, revealed a sailor blue sky.

Morning had never seemed brighter to Man-man. Glee bubbled within him. He felt it in his bones and in feet that stepped to the music in his heart.

Thrilled at what he hoped was about to unfold, he hugged his best friend, Kareem. Arms swaying, hips rolling, they twirled in a jig until, hands raised, they bumped fists.

'You're my man, bro,' said Kareem. 'We're friends for ever.'

'We're better than blood, you and me,' Man-man replied. 'We go deeper than a black hole. We fit in the here and now and in galaxies yet to come. Yah!'

They fist-bumped again and performed a routine they'd made up when they were younger, bumping everything they could: fists, knuckles, elbows, knees and heads. They clicked fingers, slapped palms and yowled like coyote pups at night.

Behind them, loitering with a gaggle of girlfriends, Pan looked away. 'Some peeps are never going to grow up,' she muttered. 'Some peeps are too far gone to have any sense whatsoever.'

Arm in arm, the boys were about to jig-dance again when a voice they knew well bellowed: 'You two. Come over here!'

Aunty Flo had taken two rails of costumes into a corner of the lock-up.

A dank hideaway under railway arches, it was where mechanics and artists in the troupe had engineered the float. It was where they'd built it and spent weekends and weekdays after hours, decorating it. Using anything they could lay their hands on, and just about everything that was donated – tinsel, cardboard, long, luxurious ostrich feathers, bolts of fabric in every colour you could think of – as well as the wheels of junkyard cars – they'd created a fantastical creature. Neither fish nor fowl, reptile, or beast, it was *magnificently* weird.

41

Aunty Flo's costumes were as far away from the float as possible. Every outfit was wrapped in plastic to keep it clean, the nametag of its wearer attached.

'Come,' she said, beckoning Man-man and Kareem.

The boys elbowed a path through a crowd of helpers to Aunty Flo.

She plucked two sets of clothes from the rack. The first was Kareem's.

When Aunty Flo turned to Man-man, a note of caution crept into her voice: 'I've put my heart and soul into this costume,' she said: 'I've sewn every stitch of it and sourced every item: hat, jacket, all off it.' She paused, looking into Man-man's eyes. It was the look that said: *I see you. I know you inside out. Pickney, I can even hear the hammering of your heart.*

'I want you to remember, Man-man,' she said, 'that when you put these clothes on, you should wear them with care and rejoice in who you become. You want your mum to be proud, don't you?'

Man-man nodded.

His mum was going to watch the carnival with Nan from the balcony at Aunty Flo's flat.

That morning had been momentous for the Baptiste family. It had been the first time Trilby had gone 'out' to more than a doctor's appointment or a hospital clinic. And, that morning, for the first time ever, Man-man had seen his mum in a wheelchair.

'I'm on the mend, Man-man,' Mum had told him. 'The wheelchair will help me get where I need to be to watch you.'

Happy yet sad at the same time, Man-man thought he'd understood.

'Mum says thank you for letting her use your balcony, Aunty Flo. Nan says thank you too.'

'It's my pleasure, sweetheart. Like I said, wear that costume as if you *mean* it. Live it, body and soul for a day.'

'I will,' came his reply.

'Good,' said Aunt Flo. 'Now shoo!'

The friends scooted to a part of the lock-up that had been screened off to make a pop-up dressing room for boys.

Man-man tore the wrapping off and then held up the coat hanger on which his costume dangled. He turned it around slowly, inspecting it from every angle.

Soft as a kitten, the clothes shimmered in the shadows of the lock-up like a dream about to burst into life.

He nuzzled them, delighted, while Kareem slipped out of his track suit into baggy black trousers. After hauling a creamy, cotton shirt over his head, he slid back into his trainers and then hitched a sword around his waist. He donned a tricorn hat, and as he adjusted a red bandana around his neck, he grinned at Man-man; a satisfied grin that said: '*This* is who I'm going to be for a day: a pirate and adventurer, a saviour of captives on the seven seas.' Then, and only then, did Kareem cover an eye with an eyepatch he'd made himself.

'Nice,' Man-man exclaimed as his friend started breathing life into his dream.

'Partner, I'm better than nice.'

'You're a hero! The king of carnival.'

'Yes, man! Say it loud and say it proud! Say it again, dude!'

Man-man repeated his words. He said them again and again. And while he praised Kareem to everyone who cared to listen, he pulled on a

leopard print leotard, a tawny blend of caramel, black and brown rosettes.

He'd asked Aunty Flo for a leotard to be part of his costume because he needed his limbs to be free to dance as he pleased: to leap and do the splits. Knowing how much he'd enjoyed the *Black Panther* movie she'd suggested one made in leopard print.

Man-man rolled his neck. Relaxing his shoulders, he wriggled into a red military style jacket. The tassels on the jacket dazzled, glowing golden as Man-man whirled around. Red was the colour of Jean-Jacques Dessalines, the first ruler of an independent Haiti. Red was also for Shango, the god of thunder and lightning, a warrior god and lord of dance.

Delighted the tassels moved whenever he did, Man-man placed a bicorn hat on his head. The hat was for Toussaint Louverture, the Father of Haiti who'd freed his homeland from slavery and fought for his nation's independence. On the hat was a single white feather.

The hat itched.

Man-man took it off, blew into it twice, and scrabbling around inside, smoothed bumps in the lining. Once the bicorn felt comfortable, Man-man looked at himself in a mirror that ran down a side of the dressing room.

He stared, and as he did, he saw the feather twitch.

He saw it quiver again.

Hand on heart, he was *sure* that was what he'd seen. He was one hundred per cent convinced. Unless...

Either the feather had fluttered, or the zig-zag-zap of the lightning flash design in his hair was beginning to pulse.

A tingling sensation rippled down Man-man's spine. His back straightened. His chin jutted out, and from one moment to the next, he felt himself become who he wanted to be: a mash-up of Toussaint and Dessalines, both mighty men, both among the greatest freedom fighters of all time.

'Way to go, dude,' whooped Kareem. 'Toussaint and Dessalines never looked better!'

The boys high-fived as they joined the queue waiting to be made up.

Ahead of them was Pan, her weave woven into an elaborate headdress of green, gold and white feathers. She had feathers of the same colour streaming from her shoulders and hips. Beneath them she wore a dazzling emerald body suit bejewelled with rhinestones.

Man-man's mouth opened. Pan looked

spectacular. And when she turned, revealing a bustle of plumes that cascaded into a train, Kareem asked: 'What's she supposed to be, partner?'

'The Sweet Bird of Freedom,' mumbled Man-man. 'I never imagined she'd ever look nice.'

'Same here,' Kareem replied.

Edging closer to his sister, Man-man touched her arm. 'Pan,' he murmured. Then, tongue-tied, overcome by her splendour, he mouthed: 'Wow!'

She gave him a rare smile, a smile that tasted of honey as a sudden rush of sister-love overwhelmed him.

'You're pretty wonderful too, lil' bro.' Lapping up his approval, Pan's eyes twinkled, widening as an idea came to her. 'Shall we give Nan something to gripe about today? Moves that will kick ass and stick in her gullet... Are you with me, lil' bro?'

'I'm with you, Pan! With you to the moon and back!'

Half an hour later, Man-man, Pan and Kareem clambered to the top deck of the float. Two other dancers were already stretching as they waited for the float to set off. Below them, Jules Baptiste was testing the sound system.

'One. Two. Three. Testing. Testing...' He fixed the speakers in place, positioning them in front of the deck he'd be using to play music. Having arranged the amplifiers for maximum effect, his hand slapped a rhythm on his thigh. Snapping the fingers of his other hand, he turned his head this way and that. Anyone who knew him could tell that he was deciding which of his favourite dance tunes he should put on to liven up the procession. A procession led by the Let Freedom Rain troupe on the top deck of the float, while those behind followed.

Dressed in white, the black star of Africa emblazoned on their chests, every child and adult on the ground moved into position, revving themselves up.

At the first blast of music, a hush descended.

'Are we ready?' Jules bellowed.

'We're ready,' everyone shouted.

'Ready? Truly ready?'

'Yes!'

And all the while, as Jules called and the troupe responded, a group of djembe drummers, drums strapped to their waists, thumped to mark the beat between Jules's call and the boisterous response.

Music soared.

Bodies moved, limbering up and stretching to hail the sky.

Feet shuffled before pumping the ground to salute the earth beneath them.

Knees, hips, shoulders, everything below and above swayed, while hands started clapping.

'Are you ready to Let Freedom Rain?' cried Jules.

'We're ready!'

'Truly ready?'

Like a dragon suddenly awake after years of slumber, with a resounding roar of: 'We're ready!' they were off.

THE THRONG at carnival was intense. People were everywhere. Tall, fat, short, slim. People as far as the eye could see. Men and women ebbing and flowing. Old and young. Black, white, every shade in between.

People strolling, chatting in different languages. People watching, eating and drinking. While others, in front of sound systems at full blast, danced, leaping up and down.

Out of nowhere, in the distance, the Freedom Dragon appeared, drummers and crew behind it. Laughter followed in their wake, as bit by bit, the dragon advanced, a glorious mess of colour and movement.

On top, below, along its swishing white tail on which the black star of freedom throbbed, the dragon trudged triumphant.

As it approached Aunty Flo's balcony, Man-man, Pan and Kareem, determined to outdo each other, displayed their best moves in a frenzy of steps. When they were close enough to see Trilby, they planned to look up and wave to her.

Pan was a bird about to soar. With a high kick and a jump, Kareem drew his sword, while Man-man gyrated, reeling in the rhythms around him.

Music pumped through his heart and soul. Happiness ballooned in him until, soaked in sound, he felt himself changing. No longer a boy, he became Toussaint and Dessalines, lords of the dance. He was the pulse at the centre of every cry for freedom and every urge to fight for it. Waving his arms, Man-man whooped at passers-by.

Pan elbowed her brother aside and took centre stage. There, feathers fluttering, she preened herself. Back bending, eyes flashing, rocking from side to side, facing this way, then that.

She dared Kareem to come closer. The moment he did, she brushed him away and sashayed to her brother. As soon as Man-man responded, she turned her back on him and, spreading her feathers for the world to see, raised her arms with the cry: 'Jump up!'

'Jump up!' replied passers-by.

'Jump up!' Pan shouted.

Enchanted by the energy on the float, a crowd gathered and followed it.

That's when the boys took over. While Pan rested, Man-man and Kareem competed with each other in a jumble of moves that combined breakdance and hip swivels. They pranced and twirled and somersaulted. One moment they were on the ground, next high in the air. Music vibrated in them, and as it did, the streak of lightning on the side of Man-man's head sizzled while his happiness swelled.

Way ahead, beyond Aunty Flo's balcony, in costumes of white and gold, a samba school paraded. Feet twirling, bodies twisting in unison, they turned again and again. Man-man saw them. He heard djembe drums pounding beneath the tinkle of steel drums. Around and about him, in the air he breathed, he savoured fragments of salsa, soca, calypso as well. From every direction, music played.

'Look at those kids,' someone shouted, pointing at the float. 'Look at them!'

Eyes swivelled, gaping at the upper deck of the dragon. Where one looked, others followed.

Within seconds, ten, twenty, fifty pairs of eyes were fixed on Man-man, Pan and Kareem. Jaws dropped as more and more people turned to gawp.

Among them, eyes, unseen in the light of a summer's day, opened and gaped, greedy to lap up the talent on display.

Feeling a shadow on his back, Man-man trembled as waves of delight rippled around him.

'Those kids are something else!'

'Isn't that Jules Baptiste's crew? You know Jules. Jules, the hair stylist...'

'Let freedom reign!' an old woman cried. 'Freedom now and for ever!'

The dragon careened in view of Aunty Flo's balcony. Man-man looked up and through a blur of images, spotted Trilby's smiling face.

He waved to her, as did Pan and Kareem. Trilby had never looked happier. Pushing her wheelchair back, she heaved herself up and leaning over the balcony, blew kisses to the children.

Pan's feathers quivered, she glided and leaped.

And when the epaulettes on Man-man's jacket whirled in a haze of red and gold, Trilby's smile, bright as a firefly, seemed to sparkle for Man-man alone.

'Make her better,' he whispered. 'Let my mum be as she was before. Please! Please!'

If you'd asked Man-man who he was pleading with, he wouldn't have been able to tell you.

His plea came from the heart. The heart of a dancer, who as he moved felt the vibration of the wooden stage beneath him. His feet tapped and slid supported by the crushed roots and trunks of trees. The more he moved, the more the stage quivered. Sensing the laughter in Man-man's feet, the lilt and bounce in his steps, memories of what it was to be alive kindled in them.

They heard an echo of the forests they'd come from. They felt the shiver of cool breezes that had once lifted their leaves. One plank of wood remembered its home so keenly, it released a trickle of tears: beads of pine sap. No wonder the scent of pine nipped Man-man's nose.

His eyes still on Trilby, Man-man asked again of no one in particular: 'Please, if you're listening, *please* make her better.'

He raised an arm to salute his mum.

As he did so,
as the crowd milled
around the float, a sudden
rush of wind surged through
carnival.

Skirts and dresses billowed.

Hats scattered.

Flecks of dust rose and fell.

It was then, and only then, that Man-man
noticed something hovering above his mum's face.
The shadow he'd felt on his back moments before
loomed large before him. It bloomed slowly, a mix
of light and dark, dust and cloud. Merging and
shifting, it seemed… Man-man gulped.
It wasn't possible.

He rubbed his eyes, convinced he was seeing things. But no! It was still there. Above his mum and a heaving mass of people, a being was taking shape. A shimmering creature with lips, forehead, chin: a mingling of blue sky and the colours of carnival.

That's the face of a warrior, thought Man-man.

It was a woman's face, blue-black in colour, hair hidden under a helmet of gold coins.

He took a step back as eyes dark as coal marvelled at him. It was those eyes which frightened him. They seemed hungry. Hungry for him.

'You called me,' the woman said. 'Didn't you ask me to help you?'

Was this the Queen of Revels? Nah. Pan had said the Revel Queen was nothing but foolishness and make-believe, while another voice whispered: 'This is for real, Man-man. Believe, Man-man, *believe*.'

He shook his head to clear it. 'Are you seeing what I'm seeing?' he asked his sister and Kareem.

Glancing in the same direction as his friend, Kareem shrugged: 'Ain't nothing to see there, partner.'

'I see it,' said Pan, grabbing Man-man's hand. 'Lil' bro, why's she looking at you like that?'

Man-man stepped back.

'What's going on, dude?' Kareem clutched Man-man's shoulder.

Inch by inch, the children retreated from the face only two of them could see.

Every time they moved, the being advanced.

Inquisitive.

Ravenous, they thought.

A giant cat staring at a litter of tiny mice while, below, Jules Baptiste shouted: 'Africa riding us, folks! She's in us! Feel her rhythm. Feel her vibe. Jump up, 'cause today all of we *Africans*!'

Moving further and further back, Man-man, Pan and Kareem slammed against the guardrail that surrounded the top deck of the float. The jolt tipped Man-man's hat off his head.

As it tumbled, another howl of wind ripped through the crowd tossing debris everywhere. In the kerfuffle that followed, beneath the gasps and cries, the coughing and spluttering, the sneezes

that shook old and young alike, the face in the sky caught sight of the bolt of lightning etched in Man-man's hair.

She saw it.

The bolt crackled, sending tingles down Man-man's spine.

The woman warrior smiled, beckoning. 'Come to me, boy. You called me. Come home!'

Kareem's grip on Man-man tightened as Pan drew him closer. 'I've got you, lil' bro. You and me, we're going nowhere!'

Even if he'd wanted to, Man-man wasn't able to move. He froze, mesmerised by the excitement in the being's eyes, the gold coins that shielded her head.

Still smiling, the woman warrior scooped him up and quickly snuffled him away.

'AAAAAAAAAHGRRRHELP! What on earth?' Pan screamed.

No one replied.

No one was able to answer her question.

How could they when the three of them were hurtling through a tunnel of wind? A wormhole, it pummelled them at the same time as it sucked and blew them along. It was as if, having been swallowed by a whale, they were travelling, twisting and turning, in its gut.

I wish this was a whale! thought Man-man. A *whale* he could understand. He'd seen pods of them on television. But *this? This* was something new.

What did the woman want and what was she?

Questions buzzing in his head, Man-man's stomach churned. His heart lurched against his ribs, as it did when riding a big dipper.

Pan's screeches pierced him again.

He squeezed his eyes shut and concentrated on breathing – a trick he'd discovered with Kareem. They'd once gone to a funfair, bought tickets for a Ferris wheel. Man-man had soon discovered that to survive the world whirling around him, he had to close his eyes. Close his eyes, be still and breathe.

Best not to see where you're heading on a trip into the unknown.

Man-man plummeted before he was thrust upwards again. Weightless, for a few seconds, he imagined he was flying, only to be shoved down a slipstream of air that had him spinning and tumbling, head over heels.

Even so, questions still fizzed in him. Questions he raised with Kareem when they talked about their latest obsessions: alien abduction, parallel universes, black holes in space. You name it, they talked about it. Was it possible that this was what was happening? Were his dad and Pan mistaken? Was the warrior woman an agent from Wakanda transporting them to a secret destination?

By now, Kareem was yelling as well. Kareem and Pan, usually so different, united. And then, whatever had snuffled them up, spat them out. That's when Man-man started howling. Eyes wide open, he somersaulted and rolled to a stop on tufts of grass.

Pan wasn't so lucky. 'Ouch,' she cried, twisting her ankle as she hit the ground. Shorn of her feathers, what was left of her weave could have passed for the torn branches of a weeping willow.

She scowled at her brother. 'This madness is doing my head in, Man-man! What's going on? What have you done?'

Uh oh. The Sweet Bird of Freedom had flown, and Pan was back to her usual self, doing what she did so well: sharpening her eyes into pinpricks of anger. 'Well?' she huffed.

A belch of thunder boomed.

Kareem plunged to the ground on hands and knees. 'What in the world was that about?'

Hat and eyepatch gone, Kareem's shirt was ripped to pieces. 'Partner, if you have something to tell us, now's the time to speak. *Spill.*'

Tempted to laugh, Man-man whimpered instead. How could he laugh when his best friend was staring at him in the same way as Pan? 'Why are you both eyeballing me?'

They wanted answers to the questions he was asking himself. 'You think I'm to blame, do you? What did I do, then? If you can't tell me what I've done, why're you guys dumping on me?'

'We're looking at you because that *thing* was staring at *you*. *You*, lil' bro. *You*, not silly old me who's sprained her ankle. That thing was after...' She jabbed Man-man in the chest, while her eyes stuck pins in him as if he was someone she wanted to jinx.

A peal of laughter rang through a cluster of casuarina and almond trees in front of them.

Immediately, the design at the side of Man-man's head twitched. He felt a twinge and looked around, as did Kareem and Pan.

Wherever they were was warm and sultry. A scent of jasmine hung in the air. Jasmine and another perfume that Man-man recognised but couldn't quite place. He sniffed. Sniffed again, savouring the smell. An image seeded in his mind of a plant with glossy, green leaves and white flowers. Where had he seen it and smelled that odour? His memory hovered, tilting to remember.

Of course! It grew at the bottom of Nan's garden in Jamaica. Myrtle. That's what she had called it. Her precious love plant, myrtle. A token of true love.

Above, a sky flecked blue and pink, was getting ready for dusk. The sun's kiss glazed almond leaves and blossoms in a dappled, golden haze. Even the brown and reddish tone of Man-man's skin seemed to glow as if lit from within.

More laughter. From a different place.

A long, glorious blast of glee as Man-man sensed the being's presence again. His heartbeat quickened. The streak of lightning on his head thrummed. But this time the thrumming came with an urge to move his body and feet, to dance until he found her.

He sprang up. His hands slapped his thighs, and then patted his elbows. His palms clashed,

clapping. He tried to press pause in his mind and reel back time, but the impulse to dance was urgent, inescapable.

He had to move.

Move and shout.

'Folks, she's here,' Man-man cried. 'Whenever she laughs, I feel her. She's close. Very close.'

'Where?' asked Pan.

Man-man pointed towards some palm trees. Beyond them was a slash of sand and a crash of waves.

'It's her. I've got to find her…'

Loud trills and giggles were followed by peels of delight from every direction.

Alive. Laughter laced with whoops of carnival joy.

'She's everywhere. Got to find her. Got to.'

'Why?' asked Pan.

'I won't be able to stop grooving until I do.' Swinging his head from side to side, Man-man clicked his fingers as if listening to music only he could follow.

'Dude, are you sure?' asked Kareem. 'Are you sure we should go after whatever brought us here?'

Man-man nodded. 'I don't have a choice.'

Pan clutched her brother's shoulders. 'Course, you have a choice!' she insisted in her loudest Big-Sister-Mistress-of-the-Universe voice.

'You have a choice, same as everyone else. *Stand* still, Man-man. Calm yourself!'

She tried to root him to the spot. She tried with all her might, but Man-man bounced from foot to foot.

'Calm down, lil' bro. *Think* before you act. And while you're at it, you'd better figure out how we're supposed to track down something that's everywhere!'

'Stick with me, Pan. That's all I'm asking.'

Man-man broke free and leaped to the roar of chuckling in his head.

'Either I find her,' he gasped. 'Or she finds

me, 'cause one way or another, the two of us are connected.'

'*Stop!*' Pan shrieked as Man-man darted away.

Kareem danced his friend back to her.

Once again, Pan hoped beyond hope that whatever gripped her brother would bend to her will. '*Chill*, bro!'

When he didn't chill, when he didn't calm himself, Pan's fear exploded. 'Man-man, you're freaking me out. I'm begging you. Enough of this foolishness.'

'He can't help himself,' Kareem told her. Draping an arm around his friend, he too began swaying to music only Man-man could hear.

Out of nowhere, Nan's words came back to haunt Pan. *'Carnival, barnacle!'*

What if Nan had been right, after all? What if Man-man, like their great-grandma, Gatsby, was in the state he was in because of carnival and the three ugly sisters of alcohol, dancing and revelry? What if they were marooned in this place because the Revel Queen had kidnapped them?

She was sure of it. Whatever was out there wasn't a friend. No way could it be a friend, because it was playing with her brother, playing with all of them by messing with their minds and jerking their strings.

'Come now, Pan.' Man-man offered her his arm. 'Follow me, that's all I'm asking. If you won't,

I can't stay here much longer 'cause this itch I'm scratching won't let me be till I find her.'

Torn over what they should do, Pan's shoulders slumped. 'You'd better be right about this,' she mumbled at last. 'We'd better find that thing and make sure she takes us home *fast*.'

PAN leaned on Man-man to ease the pain in her ankle. She laced her fingers with Kareem's and the trio set off.

Now they were on the move, the strings of the puppeteer pulling Man-man's limbs slackened and his urge to dance faded. As long as they kept going, he decided, they'd be OK.

They'd meandered across a grove of almonds. Now, due to Pan's injury, they were hobbling through an orchard of mango and breadfruit trees.

'Seems to me, we're still on planet earth, partner. Where exactly, who can say?'

Kareem's face brightened at the thought of endless possibilities as to where they might be.

'Could be we've entered another dimension,'

he said. 'An in-between space somewhere. Like a dream, perhaps. 'Cause to go from carnival to here.' He shook his head. 'No way is it possible in real time.'

'What?' Pan spluttered, scorching Kareem with a blink. 'You believe that?' Kissing her lips, she raised an eyebrow. *You too fool-fool!* her eyebrow scolded. *Boy, 'nuff of your nonsense!*

Kareem shrugged, unruffled for once. 'Think about it, Pan. Things seem the same here, but if you look closely,' he added, 'they're not. Not really.'

He stretched out his arm. Still glowing, the sun's lick on his skin was mottled. 'See?'

He placed his hand beside Man-man's. Flexed it, then turned it palm up.

On the outside their limbs looked exactly as they had before. What had changed was that now they could see energy pulsing through them as clearly as breath clouds air on a cold, winter morning. This was not normal.

'I wonder why we're different here,' asked Man-man.

No one replied.

With Pan's weight on his shoulder again, they pressed on, skirting a shrub of orange hibiscus and a flame tree in bloom.

'Here's another thing,' Man-man went on. 'Have you noticed?'

Kareem nodded. 'Yup, I have' he said. 'The sun isn't setting.'

'It's in exactly the same place as it was half an hour ago,' Man-man confirmed.

Pan, seeing the cogs in the boys' brains whirring, grunted, exasperated. She'd eavesdropped on enough of their conversations to know how fascinated they were by ideas she considered a waste of time. 'Geek alert,' she bleated. '*Bleep. Bleep.*'

'We're just thinking out loud,' said Man-man.

'Well, don't! Not today. Not now. Not when we should be concentrating on tracking that *thing* down and finding our way home. Agreed, Kareem?'

Kareem nodded. He would do and say whatever he needed to keep Pan off his back, but not Man-man.

'First off, she's not a *thing*,' Man-man said. 'A thing isn't human. Bet ya deep down she's more like you and me. Bet ya, Pan!'

The instant the words left Man-man's mouth, they snaked up the dangling branches of a casuarina, along its tendril-like leaves. They returned as an echo:

Thing. Thing. You and me.

You and me. Bet ya, Pan! Bet ya!

A gale of laughter pursued the echo. They heard her before she emerged from behind a large, silk cotton tree.

It was *her.* Barefoot, she was clothed in a flowing, indigo robe almost as dark as her skin. The helmet of coins Man-man and Pan had seen her wearing at carnival had disappeared, revealing a tangle of ebony-black curls. On her head was a crown of orange hibiscus flowers, and row upon row of pearl-like seeds dangled around her neck.

If she'd seemed gigantic before, now, even though she was tall, nearly two metres in height, she walked carefully, daintily. As she moved, she scarcely touched the ground while her perfume of myrtle, clinging to her like a cloak, spread about her.

She shimmered.

Indeed, the closer she loomed, the more unreal she became. Made up of tiny shards of brilliant light, what passed for her face, hair, feet and clothes twinkled.

No, she wasn't like them, Man-man decided. How could she be when she wafted, flickering like a sparkle of fireflies in wind? A breeze, soft and warm, gusted through her robe as she came closer. Ever closer. And like the breeze, there was nothing he could do to stop her. Not that he wanted to, because the nearer she came, the more her scent seeped into his skin, enchanting him.

Kareem and Pan backed away, but Man-man, propelled by the bolt of lightning in his hair, lurched forward.

The apparition advanced. She pointed at him, and as a flutter of sparks settled about him, Man-man glowed in a way that helped him feel the music of leaves and trees, the pulse of the earth beneath his feet. Best of all, the caress of the sun's smile on his face as the sky trembled.

'Careful, Man-man. Careful,' Pan cried, while Kareem screamed: 'Come back! No! No! Partner, don't do it!'

If Man-man heard them, he gave no sign of it. Captivated by the laughing woman, they

could only
imagine what he
was thinking. So
much so, that when she
was almost on top of him,
their jaws dropped, aghast at
what they saw next.

Man-man reached out,
touched her. And sure enough, as
his fingers dipped into the blaze of her
body, she dissolved, drifting away. Yet
when his fingers reappeared, they gleamed
with the indigo hue of her robe.

'Why did you call me?' she inquired.

'I didn't,' Man-man replied. 'I asked for help for
my mum, Trilby Baptiste. I want her back to how
she was before. Better. Completely better.'

She smiled: a teasing smile as pleasing as when
Trilby tickled Man-man's ribs. 'Don't you realise
that at carnival, a plea from the heart is a way to
summon me? I heard your call, saw your talent,
and came.'

'You saw me?'

'Of course, I saw you. We're connected, you and me. You said as much just now. And we are.'

'How?'

'You're a dancer, a reveller, a child born for masquerade. I've watched and seen your gift. Above all, I've noticed that when you're dancing, Man-man, you're able to winkle memories of life from objects long dead. So, when I heard your plea, I came.'

Man-man didn't understand what she was saying. Unable to grasp how he could 'winkle memories' out of anything, he detected a scuffle beneath her robe: a slip-sliding shuffle followed by a *miaow*.

The being flickered, fading for a moment, only to glisten the next. Light and dark shifted in her, changing again and again until, from beneath her hem, appeared a tortoise shell cat, the spitting image of Smudge.

Like a bull at a red rag, Pan thundered to Man-man's side, hobbling and limping, moving as fast as her ankle could muster. 'What are you doing with my cat?'

The woman chuckled. 'Didn't you call me a thing? What you should realise is that although I may not look like you, I know a lot more about you than you do about me.'

'As if I care! As if you'd *dare* hurt Smudge while I'm here. If... if... if you harm a single hair of her fur, I'll... I'll...'

'You'll do what?'

Her amusement shook the leaves of trees. Little pewee birds joined in, chirping, *Pee, pee.* Even Man-man and Kareem tittered as splinters of light within her vibrated and gleamed.

'I won't hurt you or your cat. I promise,' the apparition declared. 'I simply want you to understand that I can read you as easily as a scroll on my lap. How else could I have conjured this pet of yours?'

She lifted Smudge, allowing the cat to nestle in her arms before nuzzling her nose. Smudge leaped on to her shoulder and straight away the feline's fur feathered. Three hummingbirds broke free. Birds so quick and vivid they dazzled, merging with the brightness of her face.

Pan snarled, unamused. 'You're messing with us,' she said. '*Why?* Why've you brought us here? Who are you? What do you want?'

The woman flicked a finger at Pan's ankle, showering it with light. A warm flurry of air caressed her cheek, drenching her in perfume. Pan gulped. As she breathed out, relief flooded her face. She shook her foot. Shook it a second,

then a third time to make sure that what had happened had indeed come to pass.

Reluctantly, she mumbled: 'Thank you.'

'What is it you people say?' The apparition 'ummed' and 'ahhed'. 'You're welcome.'

'Nah, we're not American,' said Kareem, correcting her. He put an arm around Man-man who went on to say what Kareem was thinking.

'Where we come from, in London, we say, 'Cool. No problem. Happy to help you.'

Like a stranger learning a new language, she slowly repeated: 'Happy to help you.'

The boys nodded their approval.

Pan, on the other hand, folded her arms. 'While we're at it,' she said. 'While we're playing "nicey-nicey" and "getting-to-know-each-other", perhaps you could tell us *who* are you? And *why* you've brought us here?'

The apparition glittered, irritated. 'Didn't you hear us? Your brother summoned me.'

'Yeah, but he's a *kid*,' Pan pointed out. 'Stuff like this doesn't happen just 'cause a *kid* wants it to. Not where we come from, it doesn't.'

'I am not a kid!' said Man-man. 'I swear to you, Pan, I didn't mean to call her. It just happened. It came from here.' Man-man thumped his chest. 'She says a plea from the heart at carnival calls her. I asked for Mum to get better.'

As soon as Trilby was mentioned, Pan's anger flubbed like a tired balloon. 'I want her to get better too, lil' bro. We all do. And she will. I promise.'

Caught between hope and despair, Man-man made a choice: 'Can you heal my mum like you've just healed Pan's ankle?' he asked.

'I need to know more about her,' answered the apparition.

Man-man rubbed his ears, then his nose before moving as close to her as possible. Looking up at what passed for her face, he said: 'Ask me whatever you want, and I'll tell you what I can.'

Imagine his surprise when, in the blink of an eye, the woman grazed his forehead with her finger. Sparks flitted before his eyes, as bit by bit, Man-man sensed her riffling through his mind for information.

Memories, clear as photographs in an album, flickered in Man-man – photos he'd glimpsed of his parents on their wedding day; baby pictures of Pan and Trilby; Trilby as a child; Trilby with Nan; at school; a portrait of Trilby with Great-Grandma Gatsby. Trilby at every stage of her life.

There were images of her at carnival in Trinidad, Grenada and Notting Hill, among others of her teaching African dance at Man-man's school. African dance and drumming. Images so vivid that with every drum beat more and more

pictures surfaced from a bottomless well inside him
– a well he hadn't realised he possessed. A well that
stretched back to a time before he was born.

In every scene Trilby was laughing, always
laughing, before a final memory surfaced, taking
Man-man's breath away. In it, he saw his mum
holding him. There he was, a chubby baby,
her fingers caressing his crown. All the
while, as she tickled him, he basked
in her love; a love that sang him
lullabies each time he looked
in her eyes.

After rummaging through Man-man's store of memories, the apparition gazed intently at him. Somehow, she'd been able to peep into his soul and had seen not only the truth in him from a time before he was born, but beyond the last image, she had seen his mum's future as well. Man-man understood this, for as the woman stared, he felt waves of sadness rippling through the dappled light of her being. Without saying a word, she confirmed his worst fears.

'Mum's not going to make it, is she?' he cried. 'She's never going to get well again because there's no name for what she's got, and no medicine in the whole of this world that can cure it. The fog's too thick around her. Her voice is buried too deep. Tell me, Queen of Revels,' he said, naming her for the first time. 'What can I do to help my mum? Because if she dies, I'll have to follow her and bring her back.'

'MAN-MAN, stop your nonsense! How much stupid can you stuff into that head of yours?' Pan spoke in a voice that triggered the fiercest and most terrifying of her glares: her Boy-If-You-Mess-With-Me-You're-Dead glare as Kareem chimed in.

'Partner, you can't say stuff like that. That's mad talk, crazy talk.'

'But that's the way I feel,' Man-man replied. 'If I feel it, I say it. If Mum goes, so will I. I'll bring her back like they do in stories.'

'Stories are *make-believe*,' cried Pan. 'How many times do I have to tell you? Stories aren't *real*!'

Man-man stood tall. Tall and determined. 'Pan,

if you believe, it'll happen. How else do you think we got here? Carnival magic!'

In the rush of howls and protests that followed, in the clamour of lamentation and cries of: 'Don't be so fool-fool, Man-man! You think small boy like you can bring back the dead?'

Followed by: 'Partner, your mind so open, your brain fall out!'

In the shouting and chaos, of the four of them, only the Queen of Revels was silent. She didn't pass judgement. None whatsoever.

A westerly wind whispered through her light and shadow. It gusted gently, rearranging her form, giving the impression she was still sifting through information she'd learned from Man-man. And like a card player shuffling a pack, she was gleaning what she could.

While Pan ranted at her brother and a tear trickled down Kareem's cheek, Man-man waited for the Revel Queen to speak. 'I'm not mad,' he muttered. 'I'm not crazy. I just love her so much,

I'll follow her anywhere, that's all. That's the way I am.'

At last, the Revel Queen spoke: 'You know that your grandfather was a roots healer and priest in Haiti, don't you?'

Man-man nodded. He knew that his grandpa had been a roots man just like his dad. Emmanuel Baptiste had used the wisdom of plants and trees, sea and sky to help those who needed healing. And like his dad, he'd celebrated those who came before him who carried him all the way back to Africa. Most important of all, Man-man had grasped long ago that whenever Nan was around, no one in the family ever mentioned his grandfather.

'What's Gramps being a priest got to do with anything?' Pan quibbled. 'The old man's long dead and we never met him in any case.'

'He was a wise man,' said the Revel Queen, her sparks flashing as she collected her thoughts. 'He was one of my followers, one of the many, like your father, who understand our heritage: how it enlivens us at carnival, and reminds us who we truly are.'

'But Mum understands too,' said Man-man. 'Only last year she led our procession. Now she can hardly speak or walk. What can *you* do to make her better?'

The westerly wind whispered through the being again. She drifted away, then swished closer. Once the wind had softened, and she was able to speak, the Queen of Revels said: 'Let me make myself clear, Manman. It's almost impossible to change the future. Very few of your kind have the strength to wrestle with it and reverse its course. To have a chance of transforming what is yet to come, you must first understand the past. For your mother's sake, for the sake of your father and your family, are you willing to take on a task that others have failed?'

'Sure!' he replied. 'If it'll help Mum, I'll take on the galaxy and galaxies yet to come.'

'Hang on! Hang on!' Pan spluttered. 'What's the past got to do with our mum? What's it got to do with anything, when what she needs most are the best pills in the world, not the past?'

'Girl, don't you realise that the past lives in our bodies? We carry the past in us and often, if it brings pain, if it hurts us deeply, it can destroy us.'

Pan seethed: 'You're talking about our mum! *My* mum and my brother's. We ain't got no sad past. We're *happy* people. My mum, Trilby Baptiste is happy, I tell you! And that's the truth of it. The whole truth. Nothing but the truth, I swear! Ain't that so, lil' bro?'

Man-man wasn't so sure.

Day after day he'd sensed the fog that whirled around Trilby.

A fog which soaked up her voice and left it faint as a raindrop.

A fog steeped in illness, which was dragging her away.

A fog which had spewed up a feather.

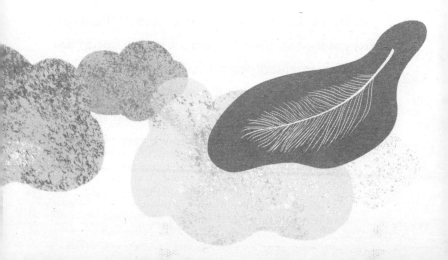

Morning and night, Man-man was aware that, even though his mum ate Nan's food, and was now as plump as a fattening pig, Trilby fretted in Nan's company.

He'd also noticed that whenever Nan was around – whether he had carnival to attend to or not – his dad disappeared.

And through it all, Man-man saw his mum's pain and felt it keenly.

'I don't know much about the past,' he admitted. 'Only the stories Dad's told me and what Kareem and I learned at our Let Freedom Rain Saturday classes. Apart from that, I can't say I know the details of our family history. Only... only...' Remembering what Nan's glare could do to him and how a glance from Pan could hurt him, he added, 'Sometimes, just a look from the women in Mum's family can slay you. Right, Pan?'

Pan nodded.

'Your mother too?' asked the apparition.

Pan nodded again as Man-man hurried on: 'Revel Queen, you've sifted my memories and shown me stuff I didn't know existed. If you're willing to help me understand what I should do, I'll do whatever it takes to change my mum's future. Are you with me, Pan, Kareem?'

With a smile and a nod Kareem accepted the challenge. Pan hesitated.

How long was her brother's quest going to take? And when would they return home again? Unused to Man-man taking the lead and loath to follow, she grunted.

Man-man nudged her: 'Come now, Pan.'

'OK,' she said. 'If going with you is for Mum, then I'm with you, lil' bro.' Turning to the Revel Queen, Pan asked a question that had been niggling her: 'Tell me, if you help us, what do you want in return?'

To her surprise, the Revel Queen replied. 'Nothing pleases me more, than a journey to find the source of a problem. And if at the same time I can right some of the wrongs done to me and my followers, it'll be worth it. Girl, are you with us?'

Pan nodded.

'Very good,' said the Revel Queen. 'Let's do it.'

THE WEST wind billowed through the Revel Queen. Her sparks scattered in the air, up, up, over the scarlet flowers of the flame tree. Slivers of light dusted blooms of a hibiscus below, while others fell on clumps of grass that started to glitter and gleam.

For a moment all was still; so quiet, in fact, that Man-man could hear the rise and fall of his breath, as well as Kareem's soft gulp as the Revel Queen disappeared. Even Pan was silent.

Nothing moved: not a blade of grass or a leaf on a tree.

Birds stopped singing, and hummingbirds, which seconds before had been flitting here and

there, sipping nectar from clumps of Bee Balm –
even the hummingbirds froze, then vanished.

Suddenly, a cloud of thunder bugs dropped from the sky.

'What on earth…?' said Pan. Her mouth opened as Man-man and Kareem gawped at storm clouds swarming above them.

The sky darkened.

Dusk turned to night and with a violent *whoosh* the roar of a tornado erupted.

It whirled around the flame tree, and as it did so, the children tumbled, faces to the ground, while the trunk of the tree writhed.

Branches snapped.

Bark and heartwood creaked.

Flowers, plucked from their stems, were flung into the air, then to the ground.

The tornado flipped and looped, circled, and shook, wreaking havoc in the glade.

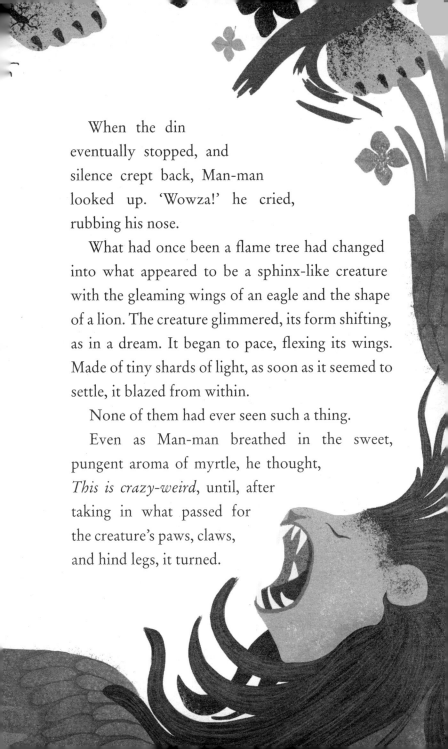

When the din
eventually stopped, and
silence crept back, Man-man
looked up. 'Wowza!' he cried,
rubbing his nose.

What had once been a flame tree had changed
into what appeared to be a sphinx-like creature
with the gleaming wings of an eagle and the shape
of a lion. The creature glimmered, its form shifting,
as in a dream. It began to pace, flexing its wings.
Made of tiny shards of light, as soon as it seemed to
settle, it blazed from within.

None of them had ever seen such a thing.

Even as Man-man breathed in the sweet,
pungent aroma of myrtle, he thought,
This is crazy-weird, until, after
taking in what passed for
the creature's paws, claws,
and hind legs, it turned.

Straight away, he recognised the face and scent of the Revel Queen. No longer a sparkle of fireflies carried by the breeze, she was a mass of dazzling, seething energy. Her crown of orange hibiscus had been replaced by the helmet of gold coins.

'It's you!' said Man-man.

Kareem gasped, while Pan, for the first time in her life, was dumbstruck. Her mouth opened and shut again and again, like a fish out of water.

The Queen of Revels laughed. 'Yes, it's me. Everything on this island is a part of me, so, I take what's mine, and become what I need to be. Now,' she continued, 'hold on tight, and I'll take you to a place where the past will be as vivid as the present.'

The Revel Queen launched herself into the sky. She whirled beyond the clouds towards the stars.

Man-man clung to her so tightly, he seemed to become a part of her. Indeed, the streak of lightning on his head crackled in such a way that as the Revel Queen soared, he felt every twitch and flex. The further she climbed, the more he sensed the sweep and thrust of her extraordinary power.

Nonetheless, even though she appeared to be made of nothing more than droplets of air and light, he felt safe, and so did Pan and Kareem. Man-man was sure of it, because the faster the Revel Queen flew, the more they became rooted in her. It was as if, by sinking into her, they were flying as well. Whether dipping or gliding, they too skimmed the sky, reeling and banking whenever she did. Moreover, speed blurred the difference between their skin and the glow of her feathers and fur. Together, they swooped, circling the contours of the earth.

Speeding through sheets of clouds, she parted them, swiping them away as she explained what she was about to do. 'We're almost there. Close to a wrinkle in time that will plunge us into Africa's past. Be patient. I'll take you to the Tree of Memories. This is a sacred tree. It will show you what you need to know, and then tell you what you must do.'

'How?' asked Man-man. 'I don't do tree-talk. Never hugged a tree in my life.'

'Boy, do you remember that crackling sensation on the side of your head when you first saw and ran to touch me? Do you remember the excitement that ran through you in my glade?'

Man-man remembered. He'd felt in tune with the world after he'd caressed the Revel Queen. Birds, trees, leaves, the ground beneath his feet, even the sky above seemed to move in step with him. It was a bit like when she'd riffled through his mind, and he'd discovered the well of memories.

'Yes, I remember,' he said. 'That's how it feels when I'm dancing – that there's more to me than just me, and it stretches way, way back.'

'Exactly,' said the Revel Queen. 'There's always more to us than meets the eye, more than what we see and touch. Bear that in mind when I take you to the Tree of Memories. And now…' she paused, banking before she merged into a funnel of wind that transported them to a completely different time and place.

HOW they got there, Man-man couldn't say. One moment he was clinging to the Revel Queen, the next he was in the branches of a magnificent iroko tree. Tall, with a wide canopy and trunk, its bark was a dark, ashen colour, the scaly skin of an ancient, grandfather tree. Its large, oval leaves dangled over Man-man's face and shoulders, hiding him in shadow. This was just as well, for the heat of the sun that afternoon was intense, the air heavy and warm.

The only trace of the Revel Queen was the scent of myrtle with its promise of love. Yet Man-man felt

121

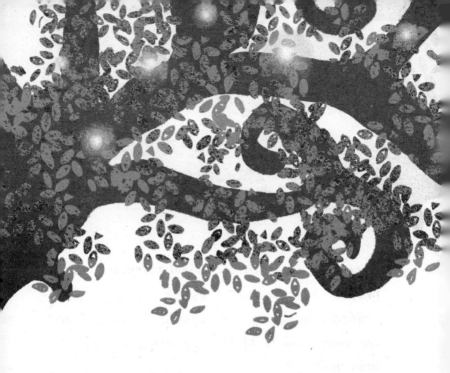

her presence. She seemed to be everywhere and nowhere in particular.

What do I do now? he wondered, as Pan and Kareem appeared beside him.

'All right, partner?'

Man-man nodded at Kareem. 'And you, Pan?'

A glint in her eye, Pan growled: 'Never felt better.'

The glint told Man-man that now they'd landed in Africa past, she didn't care to linger.

Typical Pan, he thought. *Talks tough, but has*

no taste for adventure. Not a real adventure at any rate.

Man-man shrugged as a voice boomed: 'Who are you? And what are you doing among my branches?'

The voice rattled his bones as the etching at the side of his head sizzled.

'Did you hear what I just heard?'

Pan shook her head, Kareem as well.

'I'm talking to you and you alone!' the voice thundered a second time.

'Someone's talking to me,' Man-man whispered.

Out loud, he replied: 'My name's Man-man. I'm with my friend Kareem and my sister, Pan. The Revel Queen brought us here. She said you could help me find out what's wrong with my mum, Trilby Baptiste. To understand that, I've got to make sense of the past. Only then can I wrestle with it and change her future. Isn't that so, Pan?'

Pan, rather unhelpfully, raised an eyebrow. Raised it and snorted. The glint in her eyes sparked.

'Oh dear.' The voice reminded Man-man of rolling thunder and the smell of wet earth after rain. Powerful. Old as the hills.

Man-man pressed on. 'Please can you help me? Can you reveal my family's past, my mum's especially?'

The iroko tree groaned.

Its leaves rustled, releasing a high-pitched squeak.

Its bark creaked, whining. 'Did the Revel Queen tell you my story?'

'Not exactly… she said. Um… she said…'

'Spit it out boy! A tree of my age doesn't have time to waste on truants loitering on my branches.'

Man-man trembled. He'd known from the start that his quest to help his mum wouldn't be easy. Even so, now that he was faced with the stubbornness of a grumpy old curmudgeon of a tree, he refused to give up. To fulfil his task, he needed the tree on his side.

'Sorry, Mighty Iroko,' said Man-man. 'We're not here to waste your time and play, honest, we're not. We want to go home as quickly as possible. Isn't that so, Pan?'

Pan nodded.

'No, the Revel Queen didn't tell me your story,' Man-man went on. 'I expect she thought it would be better if you told it yourself. After all, it's *your* story.'

'Well spoken, child. Perhaps once you know more about the breadth of my experience and what I can do, you'll have an idea of how best I can assist you.'

'I'm sorry, but is it possible... Would you mind very much if you spoke a bit louder? Pan and Kareem can't hear what you're saying.'

Taken aback, the tree paused. 'Are your companions not children of Shango as well? Are they not followers of the god of thunder and lightning, drumming and dance? Are they not among those able to hear and talk to me?'

'Pan's my sister and Kareem's my best friend,' said Man-man. 'The three of us love dancing. We

do, for real. In fact, we were dancing at carnival when the Revel Queen took us to her island and then brought us here. If I'm honest, Mighty Iroko, I can't say that I'm a *follower* of Shango, but I *do* have a bolt of lightning on my head.' Man-man traced the etching on his scalp with his finger. He felt the warmth of its shine, its glow of love and joy, and grinned, remembering.

'Dad designed it for me,' he said. 'My dad, Jules Baptiste. He's told me stories about Shango. Perhaps that why *I* can hear you and Pan and Kareem can't...'

The tree was silent.

A breeze whispered through its leaves unsettling them, setting them aflutter like the pitter patter of Man-man's heart.

'Maybe that's
the case,' the
tree agreed, at last.
'Thanks to your skill
and your choices, you
may have become a child of
Shango without realising it. Now,
take the hand of your friend. Take the hand of your
sister as well,' the iroko instructed, 'and they'll hear
me through the vibrations of my voice within you.
Understood?'

Man-man did as he was told. He placed his
right hand in Pan's palm, his left in Kareem's, and
together they listened to the Tree of Memories.

'Can you guess how old I am?' the sacred tree
began.

Like most relics, it was proud of how long and
valiantly it had endured.

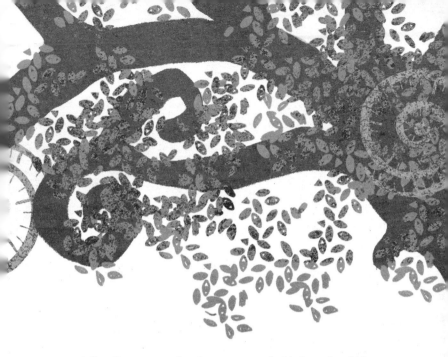

The first to reply, Pan guessed: 'A hundred?'

Kareem scratched his head. 'I reckon that you're at least two hundred years old.'

Slipping his hand from Pan's, Man-man touched the wrinkled bark of the branch he was perched on. The Tree of Memories was old. Very old. Much older than the ages of his nan and late grandfather combined. Man-man understood that some trees could live for centuries, however, its age wasn't what interested him. 'Are you older than the Queen of Revels?' he asked.

The iroko quaked, laughing.

Branches bounced.

Leaves shivered.

Bark squealed as he roared: 'Are you trying to kill me with laughter, child? Your queen is as grizzled and frayed as time itself. She's much older than her brother Shango, god of thunder and lightning. Listen carefully, boy,' the tree continued, 'wherever people have feasted and danced, whether in caves or in palaces beside the Nile and Zambesi rivers, the Queen of Revels has been with you. I'm told that at different times, you've given her all manner of names: Hathor, Shiva, Dionysus, Bacchus. No, child, I'm not that old.'

After much wheezing and cackling in twigs, bark, and heartwood, it returned to its tale.

'Five hundred years ago, when I was a sapling, I was among many. All around me was forest, and although other hardwood trees were felled, no one dared cut me down. No one dared destroy a sacred tree. A tree of spirit, a tree whose ghost, should you be foolish enough to hack it down, would first drive you mad, and then haunt your family from one generation to the next.

'I remained rooted, while my neighbours, the odum, mahogany and ebony trees of my youth, disappeared.

'The soil eroded. The sea rolled closer.

'As I grew taller and wider, as my canopy blossomed and flourished, I became the only iroko by a beach in the Bight of Benin.

'For over a hundred years, people who sheltered beneath my boughs lived, traded and died as they'd always done. Once in a while, peace was swallowed by war, but for the most part all was well, until a new wind blew from across the sea.

'They called it the fifth wind, child. A wind which brings trouble. A wind which shakes the

earth to its core and flips it upside down.'

The instant trouble was mentioned, the weight of the tree's story grazed the design on Man-man's head, kindling it. Lightning flashed, transforming words into pictures that spooled through Man-man's head as clearly as waves pounding the shore.

What he saw, his sister and Kareem did too. They may have been sitting on the bough of a tree near a beach on the Bight of Benin on the coast of West Africa, but suddenly, they heard the noise and bustle of fishermen from a bygone age; fishermen dragging their canoes ashore. They heard them singing as they hauled catches of lobsters, crabs, herrings and snappers.

'Are you listening to my story?' asked the sacred iroko.

'We're listening! We're listening,' cried Manman, as Pan and Kareem chimed:

'Yes! We're listening! We're listening too.'

'Very well,' the iroko continued. 'The earth warned us something dreadful was coming by drenching us in blood rain – a deluge of red dust from the Sahara – an omen, if ever there was one. Blood rain wept over my leaves and branches, and sure enough, before the end of that dry season, the fifth wind pitched slavers here: white men who traded in human flesh.

'Month after month, year after year, with the help of our chiefs and merchants, they marched captives to the beach ahead. There, they rowed them to ships that carried them to captivity.'

Repelled by images that unravelled before him, Man-man was tempted to close his eyes. He didn't in case he missed something vital: an ancestor of his mum or dad. A clue to his mum's illness. A scrap of evidence, a glimpse of someone, *anyone* who might help him understand the past so he could transform his mum's future.

While her brother searched for clues, Pan gritted her teeth, enraged. Unable to bear what she was seeing, she tore her hand away, horrified.

'Mighty Iroko,' she cried, as tears streamed down Kareem's face.

'We know this story already. There's no point taking us back to when we were enslaved. It's history. Enough already! Enough, I say!'

'But what if we see something that helps Mum, Pan?'

Pan shook her head, spiking Man-man with the wrath in her eyes. She was about to launch herself from the tree, but its branches and leaves, cradling her, held her in place.

'Children,' said the iroko, 'I'm telling you this story because the Revel Queen brought you to me for a reason. Be patient. Hear me out. What you must understand is that before the captives left for lands across the sea, before they departed never to return, they walked around me three times. Thrice they were made to circle my trunk in the belief that by the third time any memories they had would fade as dust in a squall. Chiefs, merchants and slavers hoped that once their captives were bound by my power, having walked around me, they'd become as pliant as tree sap.

'That's why they also call me the Tree of Forgetfulness, children. The Tree of Oblivion, a tree for wiping the past away. Day after day, month after month for centuries your ancestors walked beneath me. I hold their memories.'

The streak of lightning on Man-man's head pulsed, and once again images of what had happened reeled before him. Only this time, he was in the thick of it. Hidden by the leaves of the iroko, he sensed waves of unhappiness rising. Wave upon wave of desolation and curses as he watched a never-ending stream of prisoners girdle the trunk of the iroko.

He heard them muttering and praying, howling, protesting, begging the gods they believed in for deliverance. Their cries and whispers billowed up the tree's branches into its canopy before they were swept out to sea.

Slipping her hand into Man-man's again, Pan rejoined her brother and Kareem. The trio watched and listened, eager to hear what the ancient tree would say next.

Its voice rumbled, dipping deeper still, as if what it was about to reveal was beyond words.

'The pain of the captives was such that as they offered up their hopes and dreams, uncertain of the future; as they watered my roots with tears and remembered the past, their desolation tunnelled through the tips of my leaves, and became a part of me.

'What no one knows, except for you and the Revel Queen, is that I stored their thoughts of family and home. Their recollections of laughter at weddings, births and funerals. I gathered it all in. All of it: music, dance, festivals and stories. I hoarded them in the bark and heartwood of my trunk, in my branches, and the cells of my leaves.

'This is my story, children. I can help you understand the past because I'm a treasure trove of memories. Come in and see.'

THE TREE OF MEMORIES sank into itself. Its branches crackled, embracing Man-man, Pan and Kareem. Its leaves trembled, flinching, as if sensitive to touch.

Man-man gripped his best friend and sister.

He sensed a shift taking place, and like a car changing gear, imagined himself moving faster and faster. Closing his eyes, he steadied his breathing.

Thunder rumbled.

Lightning streaked the sky, revealing scudding rain clouds. Clouds, which looped as if dancing to drum-peals of thunder.

'Shango,' Man-man whispered.

Kareem squeezed his hand in

142

reply, and as day turned to night, the scent of myrtle bruised their nostrils. Each of them smelled her before Man-man spoke her name:

'Revel Queen, Revel Queen,
Queen of carnival,
Show me the key to my mother's past!
Revel Queen, Revel Queen,
Empress of the dance,
Heal my mother at last!'

'Think of her,' the Revel Queen crooned. 'Hold her fast in your mind and when the time's right, talk to her as if she's with you. With love such as yours, she'll hear you no matter where she is.'

Man-man held his breath as a leaf brushed his forehead. Of the memories stored in its cells, one in particular leaped out. Sure enough, a scene unfurled.

He saw an old woman. A limping, bedraggled woman trailing captives around the tree's trunk. She shouted, crying to anyone who would listen that her granddaughters must be freed.

'How am I to live without them?' she wailed.

'You've taken my sons, my daughters. You've taken their wives and husbands. Leave these two, at least, to look after me as my eyes fade. Let them stay for my sake. Or take me as well.'

The children in question were sisters. About the same age as Pan, the younger one clung to her grandmother, trying to soothe her. Holding her up, caressing her, she wept while the older girl, her eyes glazed, seemed dazed: unreachable.

'Please don't take them,' the old woman pleaded. From their nest in the Tree of Memories no translation was needed for the children to understand her. Gestures and emotions from a different time and place seized them, demanding their attention.

Man-man craned his neck, leaning as far out as he could without being seen.

The crone seemed familiar. If only she'd turn around, perhaps he'd recognise her face. She'd travelled far: her clothes were torn, the soles of her feet cracked, creased with dirt. To Man-man's dismay, her cries were met with jeering shrieks.

Slavers, white and black, those guarding prisoners and herding them to boats, hooted at her.

Yet she continued, begging for the freedom of her granddaughters. She pleaded, until one of the guards struck her with the butt of his musket, tossing her to the ground.

The children gasped.

'What?' Pan protested. 'That's totally out of order!'

'If I could, I'd smash him to mush,' said Kareem.

'Smash him!' said Man-man.

'Smash him! Smash him!' the trio chorused as the bolt of light on Man-man's head crackled and hissed in fury.

Whether their chant made any difference to what happened next, no one can say. Defiance streaked

through the woman. Kindled with thunderlight, her worn clothes burned red. First, she rubbed dirt on her face and arms. Then, lithe as a cat, she sprang up.

Pointing a finger at her attacker, she cried: 'You think because I'm old, you can take what's mine and throw me away like plantain peel? You think because I'm old and can barely see, I will bow to you? Watch me and see what is due to you and your kind.'

She raised her hand, summoning strength from her gods.

The gesture zipped through Man-man, confirming his belief that the two of them were connected. He fizzed from head to toe. Beside him, Pan, leaning out of the tree, swivelled for a better view.

The crone rained curses on the slavers, calling on the spirits of sea and sky, and the warrior god, Shango, ruler of thunder and lightning, to do her bidding.

The men laughed. They couldn't help but laugh.

Undaunted, she stood tall. Her defiance bloomed. And as it did, she grew taller and taller until she stood a giantess among pygmies.

Her gods had heard her, for when the woman raised her hand a second time, her anger was such, it slashed a seam between earth and sky, and the heavens opened.

The sea raged.

Lightning dashed the afternoon sky, and rain, fat and hard as pebbles, smashed the ground.

'You will not take my granddaughters,' hissed

the old woman.
'You will not
take them!'

Aware that the children
were about to jump down to help her, the Tree
of Memories clenched its branches, holding Man-
man, Kareem and Pan captive.

'The past has passed,' said the tree. 'Hold still
and watch.'

Advice the Revel Queen confirmed: 'Wait, Man-
man. When the past is ready to speak to you, you'll
know exactly what to do.'

Like a fighter waiting to attack, Man-man held
back.

The longer he tarried, the more the old
woman reminded him of Nan: how she
became larger when irritated; how her
words cut to the quick like a knife to the
bone. And her eyes? Why didn't the old
woman turn around, so he could see
her face clearly? 'Turn,' he pleaded.
'Then Mum can watch the past
unravel through me.'

The thought flickered as the woman's fury erupted.

The chains binding captives shattered, and one after the other, guards tumbled to the ground, repelled by her power.

'Watch out!' Kareem screamed.

A slaver with a musket was taking aim.

'Behind you! Behind you!' cried Manman and Pan.

The commotion below hobbled their

voices, even as they heard the woman cackling. Then she turned around.

'Mercy me!' said Pan, using one of Nan's favourite expressions. 'Nan? What's our nan doing here?'

Man-man smiled at his sister. 'If she wasn't so black it could be her. Could be, but it ain't. She's our ancestor, Pan.'

'Wicked!' For once Pan and Kareem agreed.

Silently, Man-man spoke to the part of Trilby he carried with him everywhere: *I hope you're watching, Mum. I knew it. I knew the old woman and I were connected. The Tree of Memories is showing me how your sickness started. Look!*

I'm looking, son!

Raising her arm a third time, the old woman wrapped herself in swathes of sea mist. It swirled about her as she touched the forehead of the eldest of her granddaughters.

'They've broken you, child,' she said. 'They've drained you like water from a calabash. Be brave, your suffering is over.'

With a click of her fingers, she transformed the girl into an egret. An egret that soared into the sky the moment the musket fired.

Flabbergasted, Pan opened and shut her mouth as more egrets followed the first. 'The Sweet Bird of Freedom,' she muttered, remembering the plumage of her outfit for carnival. 'Let Freedom Rain!' she cried, clutching her little brother.

'Told you,' he replied. 'Magic is real. It happens.'

Sure enough, in the blink of an eye, captives, suddenly free, feathered, grew wings, and flying higher and higher, escaped while Man-man, and the mum he hugged to himself, watched.

In the thickening fog of musket fire and sea mist, the old woman clasped her youngest granddaughter. 'Ayodele,' she said. 'From the moment you opened your eyes and I saw what you're made of, I loved you. You are one of mine: a girl with the will to wield a machete in her eyes. If these slavers had not

destroyed our kingdom, you would have become a woman warrior, a shield maiden to our queen.'

The old woman hugged Ayo.

The girl clung to her. 'Take me with you,' she begged. 'Either kill me or set me free!'

'You will live, joy of my heart. You will live with the most precious of my gifts: the ability to slice and dice your enemies with a glance. You will pass this on to your daughters, and they, in turn, will

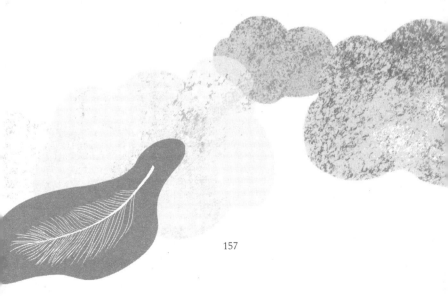

give it to their daughters to help them endure the strange land these traders are taking you to. They trade in flesh and bone. You will fight them with Shango's power, the machete hidden in your eyes.'

Distraught, Ayo cleaved to her grandmother. The old woman shook her off but when the girl still clung to her, energy pulsed through her, and Ayo fell to her knees.

'Joy of my heart,' said her grandmother, 'fate

decrees that I leave you here. When I'm gone, look up into the branches of this sacred tree. There you will see your future.'

Another shot sounded. Then three and four.

In the mayhem, as more egrets took to the sky and whips slashed the backs of those left behind, Ayo turned, and looking into the branches of the Tree of Memories, saw the shining faces of three children.

'Mum,' cried Man-man, amazed at how much the girl below resembled Trilby. 'It can't be you, but it's you! It's you!'

'It's me, Panama!' Pan screamed.

'She looks like your mum, but you know it's not, right? This is the past. Or am I missing something?' asked Kareem.

Man-man didn't care. Desperate to touch his ancestor who, apart from having the dark skin of his dad, was identical to his mum in so many ways, he scrambled forward.

When he still couldn't reach her, with Kareem holding his feet, he inched further along the branch. 'Ayo! It's me. It's me! I'm your future,' he shouted.

The girl's brow furrowed.

She called to Shango for help. She muttered a hurried incantation, a spell to fly away to join her sister and grandmother. When the charm failed her, in tears, she coughed up the silky, white feather of an egret.

If only I could get closer, thought Man-man.

If he touched her, his mum would be touching her too. If they brushed their fingers over hers and held her hand, he believed that the fog that whirled around Trilby, the same fog of despair that had dragged her back to this moment in time, would

clear, and she'd get better.

Ignoring Kareem's calls to be careful, Pan's pleas to stop, Man-man crept along the branch, commando-style.

'Ayo! Ayo!' he called, speaking to his past.

Ayo looked up again, and recognised, through her tears, a descendant just as her grandmother had said. Her future in the shape of a determined, courageous boy with the same sloping forehead as hers, and a face brimming with love.

'You're not alone,' Man-man cried. 'We're with you. We won't forget you. Because now I've seen you and my mum has witnessed what happened to you, she's going to get better. I know she will.'

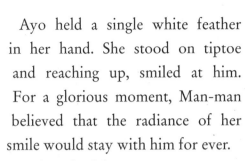

Ayo held a single white feather in her hand. She stood on tiptoe and reaching up, smiled at him. For a glorious moment, Man-man believed that the radiance of her smile would stay with him for ever.

With a final heave, Man-man was stretching to touch her and accept her gift, when the branch he was on broke.

HE'D TOUCHED her. He'd grazed the tip of Ayo's forefinger and grabbed the feather just before the branch collapsed and she was hustled away.

Tumbling, twisting and turning, Kareem and Pan clinging to him, Man-man heard a trill of delight in one ear, and in the other, cries of shock and horror.

Waves of love wrapped around him, assuring him that no matter what happened, or where he landed, he'd be fine. With the bolt of lightning on his head, and the Revel Queen at his side, he was confident that for as long as he drew breath, he'd use his talent to celebrate carnival.

'Dad. I'm a roots man too! I've been to Africa past and seen our ancestors. I've seen Ayo! A girl who wields a machete in her eyes. Same as Pan, Mum and Fedora. Mum, are you still watching? Can you still hear me?' he asked, as a westerly wind swept the trio across the river of time.

On this occasion, Man-man, his eyes wide open, relished the voyage. There was so much to see, so much to enjoy in the twilight world of shadows and stars they were plunging through.

'The past spoke to me, Dad,' he continued. 'Thanks to the Tree of Memories, Mum's remembered. She's going to be fine. I'm sure of it. Through me, she saw Ayo and her grandmother. We saw captives turn into birds and fly to freedom. You're going to get better, Mum. You're going to get better.'

These were the thoughts that zipped through Man-man.

Thoughts interrupted by the voice of the Revel Queen. 'You've done well, child. Now, watch and see.'

She pulled him back to the moment when, catching sight of her face at carnival, he'd inched back on the Let Freedom Rain float. Man-man remembered wanting to get as far away from the apparition as possible.

Now, looking from above, he saw himself retreat on the platform, Pan and Kareem either side of him. He saw fear glaze his face as his back slammed against the guardrail on the top deck of the float.

The first jolt tipped his hat off.

What he hadn't realised was that in this version of events, the screws that held the banister in place were loose and the more he leaned against it, the looser they became. Until, under the weight of the three of them the railing gave way and, slowly, slowly, they tumbled to the ground.

'Listen,' said the Revel Queen.

From the balcony, his mum's scream pierced Man-man like a knife through butter. Having seen them fall, to the surprise of everyone who knew how ill she was, Trilby thrust her wheelchair aside, and ran downstairs faster than Wonder Woman. Out of the front door, she elbowed her way through the carnival crowd.

'Man-man, are you all right?' she cried.

Her voice, loud as a foghorn, parted the crowd. 'We need help here. Quickly! Quickly!'

Looking down on himself, Man-man noticed that he was struggling to sit up.

'Stay still!' Trilby bellowed. 'Don't move. You mustn't move until someone's checked you out. Pan, are you all right? And you, Kareem?'

Pan had sprained her ankle, while Kareem, shaking his head the better to clear it, nodded.

'Will I see you again?' Man-man asked the Revel Queen. This, the first of many questions he wanted answers to, was followed by a second: 'Will Ayo be all right? Will she endure?'

'You told me when you first touched me that we're connected,' the Revel Queen replied. 'You're now a traveller through time and space, a boy with the courage to shape the future by soothing the scars of your family's past.'

'But did she? Did Ayo *really* endure?'

'Your existence is proof that, somehow, she did. Now, go home, Man-man. Your task is done.'

Man-man sat up, amazed at how two faces born at different times, in different places could look so similar. The likeness between Ayo and his mum had been striking. They had the same heart-shaped face, the same dark, flashing eyes. One moment sharp as flint, then tender with love.

Trilby pressed her forehead against Man-man's, and in that moment, as he felt the rush of her tears on his cheeks, he sensed her relief.

He fumbled in his pocket for the gift Ayo, his ancestor had given him. The feather was no longer there.

'There's no need to show me,' his mum said. 'I saw it. You helped me see her. You've helped me recover what would have been impossible without you. Thank you, Man-man. Thank you!'

It had worked.

In days to come, older, 'wiser' heads would say that Trilby's spectacular improvement was due to the shock of seeing the three of them fall. But that afternoon, Pan and Kareem and Man-man especially, disagreed. Trilby was walking and talking again. How long she'd be better, Man-man didn't know. What mattered was that for the time being the fog that had almost buried her, had lifted. The fog of musket fumes and sea mist that had silenced her voice had gone. Her eyes were sharp and alert, and in them Man-man saw the glint of Shango's axe. Trilby was more alive now than ever.

While his mum called for a doctor, and Jules, Aunty Flo

and the rest of their crew joined in, Kareem nodded at Man-man.

'Seems we did it, partner,' he said.

'We sure did, though whether anyone will believe us, I doubt it.'

'It certainly ain't make-believe,' said Pan. 'And never forget, without me, you two would have hashed it up completely.'

'*Bleep! Bleep! Bleep!* Trigger warning!' Man-man and Kareem chanted. 'Big sister alert! Big sister alert!'

Normally, Pan would have glared at them. This time, however, she smiled, saying in her Big-Sister-Knows-Best voice, 'Well, I guess peeps like us, peeps who believe in the magic of carnival, are never going to grow up, are we?'

Man-man and Kareen laughed. 'Preach, sister! Preach!' they hollered as the three of them slapped palms and hugged.

Half an hour later, they were on
Aunty Flo's balcony dancing as they
watched the procession. Trilby clapped
her hands. Man-man, Kareem and Pan
cheered, clapping even louder. Together
they created a pattern of slaps, claps, and
fist bumps to enliven the revellers.

Soaking up the rhythms around him,
rhythms so powerful that even Nan was forced
to join in, Man-man in his groove, moved to the
sound of carnival.

Nan shook her shoulders, wiggling her hips.

Man-man saluted her. And when a whiff of
myrtle nibbled his nose, he grinned, content that

177

his dream had come true. The Queen of Revels was everywhere, yet nowhere in particular. Now he knew that whenever he snapped his fingers; whenever glee bubbled in his bones and he felt that sizzle of excitement in his feet that stretched way, way back; whenever music pulsed through his heart and soul, she was with him.

Samuel Mihaye

YABA BADOE

is a documentary filmmaker and writer. She was born in Ghana and now lives in London with her husband. Her debut novel, *A Jigsaw of Fire and Stars*, was Branford Boase shortlisted. Her third novel, *Lionheart Girl*, was Jhalak Prize longlisted and Edward Stanford Children's Travel Book of the Year shortlisted.

'Man-man's love of dance and movement gripped me at the start of his story and propelled me to the end. Now more than ever, I'm convinced it's the pulse and rhythms of Africa which make carnival so special.'

Kingsley Ohuka

JOELLE AVELINO

is a Congolese and Angolan illustrator
who grew up in the UK and lives in London.
She has a BA in illustration with marketing
from the University of Hertfordshire. She
has worked on several books including
Hey You! by Dapo Adeola.

'Yaba's mesmerising storytelling is full of the
essence of carnival from beginning to end.
I've loved bringing her words to life, capturing
the movement and magic of the story in
my illustrations.'

'A people's art is the genesis of their freedom'
Claudia Jones, founder of the Notting Hill Carnival.

I am grateful to many people for their help with *Man-man and the Tree of Memories*. First of all, my thanks to the George Padmore Institute for planting the seed of a story about carnival in my imagination and opening their archive to me. Special thanks to Nicole Moore, and to Sarah Garrod, the archivist at the Institute, whose scans of carnival paraphernalia were invaluable.

Jane Ripley, a designer of carnival floats, helped me understand their structure and design. Thank you, Jane, for your patience! Thanks also to Yinka Williams, a lover of carnival. Yinka, your photos and videos of bands in the Caribbean and Britain helped enormously. Thank you for correcting my patois!

Finally, a huge shout-out to the amazing team at Zephyr, Jessie Price, art director extraordinaire, illustrator, Joelle Avelino, and my editor, Fiona Kennedy. Joelle, it's been a joy working with you. Jessie, your vision is phenomenal. Fiona, without your ingenuity and publishing acumen, this story wouldn't have seen the light of day. Thank you for stepping in when I needed you most, and for having faith in Man-man's story. Thank you, plenty!

Yaba Badoe
London
July 2023